Brown Bear Wood

Grand Old Oak

and the Birthday Ball

Poems by
Rachel Piercey

Illustrated by
Freya Hartas

MAGIC CAT PUBLISHING

MAGIC CAT PUBLISHING

A catalogue record for this book is available from the British Library.

ISBN 978-1-913520-85-4

The illustrations were drawn in pencil and coloured digitally
Set in Bentham, La Parisienne, Lancelot and Sevillana

Published by Rachel Williams and Jenny Broom
Designed by Nicola Price and Maisy Ruffels
Edited by Helen Brown

Manufactured in China

1 3 5 7 9 8 6 4 2

FSC
www.fsc.org
MIX
Paper from
responsible sources
FSC® C104723

Welcome friends and settle in:
there's lots to do and see
as I tell you the story
of our oldest, wisest tree...

SPRING BRINGS NEW BEGINNINGS
HOW OLD IS OAK?

It started when I wondered,
as I never had before:
How long has Oak been growing here?
A hundred years, or more?

It must, I thought, take many years
of water, air and light
to spread to such a wondrous width
and such a mighty height.

What to spot around Grand Old Oak

- **BEAR** and his friends measuring Oak's trunk
- **BUNNY** counting the growth rings on a tree stump
- **PAPA BEAR** enjoying a very sleepy breakfast
- A tree with **PINK BLOSSOM** and a tree with **WHITE BLOSSOM**
- Two **SKUNKS** wearing pyjamas
- A spotty **TEAPOT**
- **PAPA MOUSE** reading aloud
- **MAMA PIGEON** and **PAPA PIGEON** with their beaks full of twigs
- A ringing **ALARM CLOCK**
- Three sleeping **SNAILS**, snuggled up together
- **MAMA DEER** with a tape measure
- A bright **MORNING STAR**
- Baby **CHIPMUNKS** brushing their teeth
- **FROG** having a big stretch
- **PROFESSOR OWL** heading for bed
- **BEAR'S LITTLE BROTHER** and **SISTER** learning how to tell the time
- Five cosy **NESTS**

HELLO, OAK!

And so, when Oak woke up again –
as catkins buzzed with bees
and seven hundred thousand buds
unfurled their glossy leaves –

I asked, "Please could you tell me
when you first began to grow?"
And Oak replied, "I sprang up here
five hundred years ago."

What to spot as Oak wakes up

○ BEAR comparing a tiny acorn to mighty Oak

○ The SQUIRREL FAMILY munching on the last of their winter hoard

○ GRANDMA BAT and GRANDPA BAT under a blanket of loose bark

○ BUNNY and MOLE exploring Oak's trunk

○ PROFESSOR OWL teaching a lesson on trees

○ The number 500 written in BLUEBELLS

○ Six hungry CATERPILLARS

- A cloud of **POLLEN**
- **SPIDER** making herself a home
- A column of **ANTS**
- **FROG** leading a science class
- The **FAWNS** with an oak sapling they've been looking after
- Seven **BEES** feasting on Oak's catkins
- A shaft of spring **SUNLIGHT** beaming through the branches
- Three **YOUNG OAK TREES** growing from the woodland floor
- **WOODPECKER** knocking on Oak's trunk
- **SNAKE** wearing a bonnet

SUMMER BRINGS GRAND IDEAS
BEAR PLANS A PARTY

I thought of all that Oak had seen;
how steady, still, it stands.
And from my hazy daydreams,
I began to form some plans...

"My friends," I said, "may I suggest
a secret birthday ball?"
They answered me with roars and cheers,
agreeing, one and all!

What to spot as Bear plans a party

- BEAR sharing his ideas
- The FOX CUBS falling over in excitement
- MAMA DEER and PAPA MOUSE starting their to-do list
- Half of MAMA WEASEL
- Five PICNIC HAMPERS
- BEAR'S LITTLE BROTHER and SISTER throwing leaf confetti
- MAMA FOX with two baskets of foraged leaves and berries
- FROG croaking extra loudly in delight
- Half of SNAKE

- CHIPMUNK sneaking off with a big slice of cake
- BUNNY hopping with happiness
- Sixteen stripy BEES
- BABY MICE picking berries
- SPIDER weaving a very special web
- A choir of BIRDS singing with joy
- NANA RABBIT and PAPA BEAR looking through a recipe book
- Ten WILD MUSHROOMS

INVITATIONS BY AIR

I wanted all of Brown Bear Wood to join the celebrations, so we created piles and piles of homemade invitations:

Please join us for a special day to mark five hundred years.

And then we sent them out with lots of helpful volunteers.

What to spot in Oak's canopy

- BEAR handing out invitations
- A group of GRASSHOPPERS making music as they wait their turn
- The RACCOON FAMILY folding RECYCLED PAPER into envelopes
- PROFESSOR OWL with a very long list
- Six SPIDERS swinging on silken threads
- Three distracted CATERPILLARS
- Nine fluttering BUTTERFLIES

PARTY

POST

- SQUIRRELS and CHIPMUNKS making invitations
- The PIGEON FAMILY setting off together
- Five tiny HOUSES

- BEAR'S LITTLE BROTHER and SISTER with a book of pressed leaves
- Seven sleeping MOTHS, waiting until nightfall
- Four INVITATIONS hanging on a line

- Three fluffy CLOUDS
- Some very strong ANTS
- Young, green ACORNS
- Four leaping CRICKETS

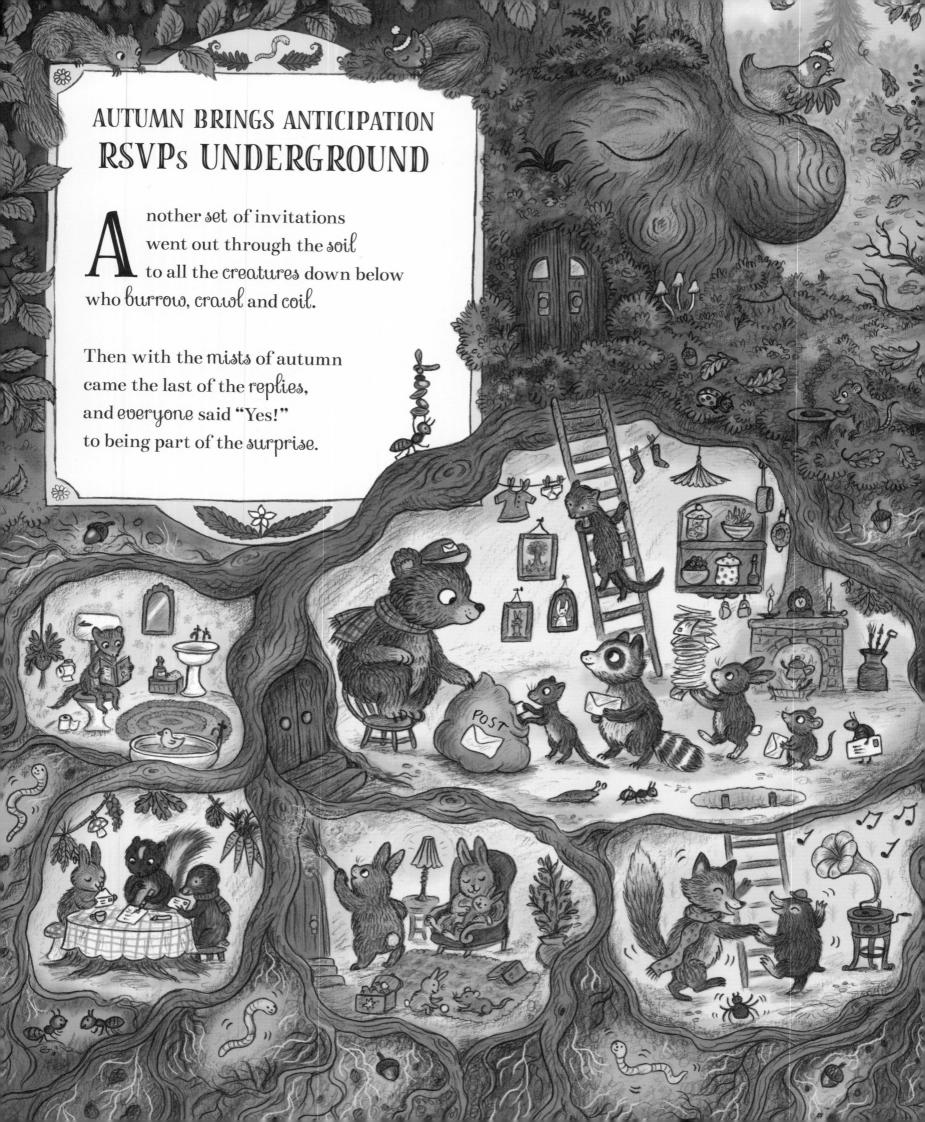

AUTUMN BRINGS ANTICIPATION
RSVPs UNDERGROUND

Another set of invitations
went out through the soil
to all the creatures down below
who burrow, crawl and coil.

Then with the mists of autumn
came the last of the replies,
and everyone said "Yes!"
to being part of the surprise.

What to spot as Bear collects RSVPs

- **BEAR** perched on a tiny chair
- Two **MILLIPEDES** munching on dead leaves
- Long, white threads on Oak's **ROOTS**
- **BUNNY** with a pile of RSVPs
- Eight buried **ACORNS**
- **ANT** with a tottering tower of seeds
- A **FALLEN BRANCH**
- **FOX CUB** and **FROG** ticking off names from the guest list
- Two yummy **APPLES**
- **PAPA RABBIT** tidying the family warren
- **MOLE** digging a tunnel
- Eight wriggling **EARTHWORMS**
- **GRANDPA TOAD** and **SNAKE** keeping cosy in a pile of leaves
- **SLUGS** and **WOODLICE** queuing to post letters
- Five different types of **FUNGI**
- A miniature **OAK TREE**
- Three **MOLEHILLS**

PRESENTS AND PREPARATIONS

I planned this ball to show Old Oak
our gratitude and care
and this included making things
to give, display and share:

confetti, banners, cards and cakes,
bouquets of odds and ends,
a collage showing Oak and me,
the very best of friends.

What to spot among the preparations

- **BEAR** making a special picture as a gift for **OAK**

- **MICE** and **CHIPMUNKS** sewing bunting

- **BUNNY** painting a picture of something **OAK** loves

- **MAMA RABBIT** and **PAPA RABBIT** making a birthday banner

- **SKUNKS** arranging dried leaves and flowers

- **BEAR'S LITTLE BROTHER** and **SISTER** stirring fruit cake batter

- The **SQUIRREL FAMILY** making jams and pickles

- **CHIFFCHAFF** licking the jam spoon

- **BABY WEASELS** writing a story for **OAK**

- **PAPA BEAR** carrying boxes of old decorations

- The **FAWNS** bottling up **OAK'S** favourite drink

- **FROG** and **SPIDER** preparing birthday cards

- **PAPA MOUSE** handing around refreshments

- Six steaming mugs of **HOT CHOCOLATE**

- A decorated **PAPA DEER**

- The **PIGEON FAMILY** creating petal confetti

- **PROFESSOR OWL** composing a poem

COUNTING DOWN THE DAYS

I wished that time would hurry up:
how hard it was to wait!
But then again, we had a lot
to sort before the date:

supplies to gather; gifts to wrap;
a whole new play to write;
a schedule for the day itself,
for morning, noon and night.

What to spot as the day draws closer

○ BEAR gathering ideas for a play all about OAK TREES

○ BUNNY and two FOX CUBS making the party schedule

○ SQUIRRELS and SKUNKS writing birthday cards

○ GRANDMA BAT and GRANDPA BAT folding napkins

○ CHIPMUNKS creating their own wrapping paper

○ MAMA DEER and PAPA MOUSE ticking off their to-do list

○ The FAWNS counting a pile of borrowed cutlery

○ Three BABY MICE trying on outfits

The **PIGEON FAMILY** washing reusable straws

PAPA BEAR teaching **BEAR'S LITTLE BROTHER** and **SISTER** how to tie a bow

The **WOODLAND BAND** rehearsing

BABY SQUIRRELS sorting reusable plates, bowls and cups into piles

Fifteen wrapped **PRESENTS**

GRANDPA TOAD and **WOODPECKER** getting tangled up in bunting

MAMA FOX and the **WEASEL FAMILY** painting scenery for the play

PAPA RACCOON and **NANA RABBIT** making costumes for the play

AUTUMN LEAVES falling from the trees

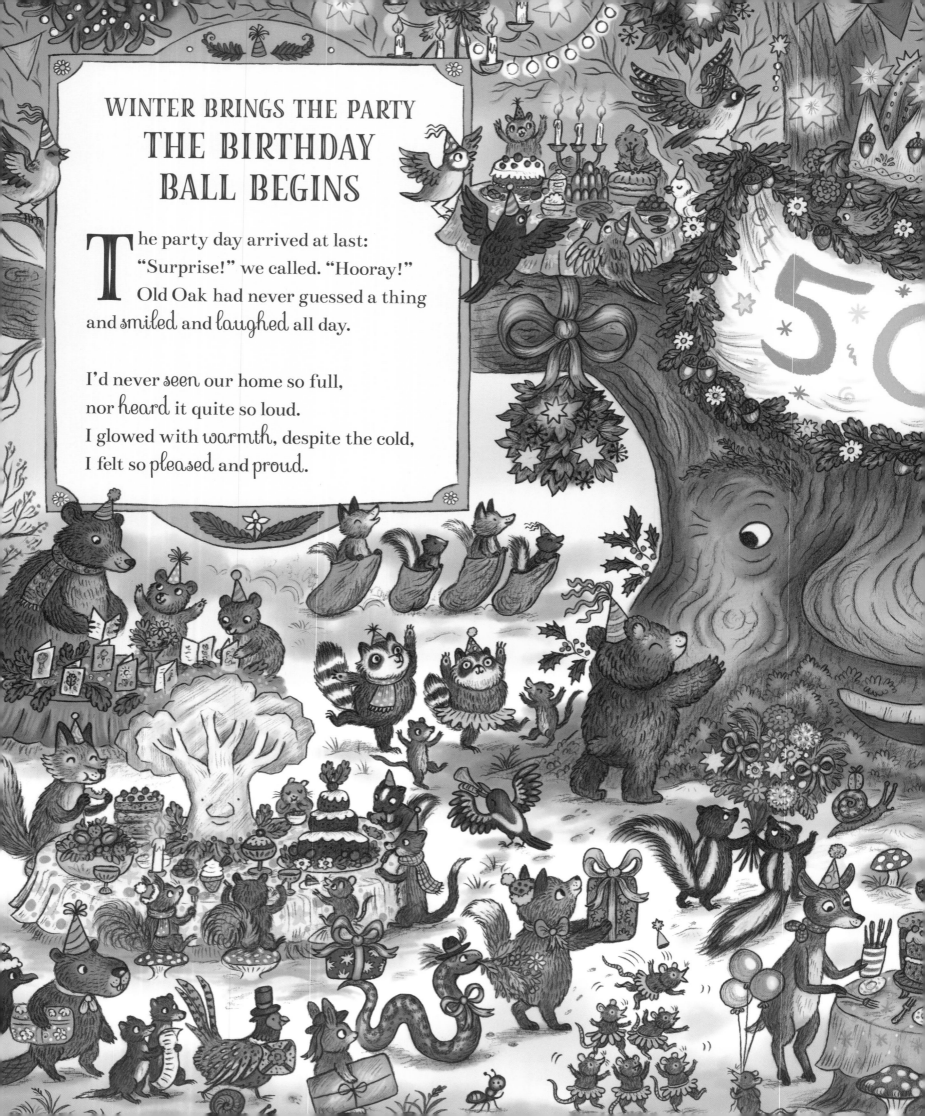

WINTER BRINGS THE PARTY
THE BIRTHDAY BALL BEGINS

The party day arrived at last:
  "Surprise!" we called. "Hooray!"
Old Oak had never guessed a thing
and smiled and laughed all day.

I'd never seen our home so full,
nor heard it quite so loud.
I glowed with warmth, despite the cold,
I felt so pleased and proud.

What to spot as the birthday ball begins

- BEAR hugging OAK
- A huge BIRTHDAY BANNER
- A long, lively QUEUE
- An ACORN-AND-SPOON race
- RACCOONS and MICE playing musical statues
- A game of APPLE-BOBBING
- A huge pile of PRESENTS and CARDS
- PAPA RABBIT and MAMA SQUIRREL hanging the last of the decorations
- A tumbling pyramid of MICE
- BUNNY and the FAWNS helping to lay out the feast
- A majestic CROWN
- FOX CUBS and SKUNKS in a sack race
- PROFESSOR OWL and PAPA RACCOON greeting guests
- Seven laden TABLES with colourful tablecloths
- A game of PICK-UP STICKS
- An ICE SCULPTURE
- PAPA BEAR placing OAK'S cards on display

IN HONOUR OF OAK

The evening finished with a play:
a story, told in rhyme,
of oaks and their significance –
today, and back through time.

We'd put it all together
as a way to honour Oak,
and played our parts with gusto
in the swirls of golden smoke.

What to spot in the play's performance

- BEAR performing his lines
- An ACORN, CATKIN and BUTTERFLY ballet
- PROFESSOR OWL dressed as a famous writer
- Fifteen glowing LANTERNS
- Two OAK BARRELS with bushy tails
- A pot of INK made from acorns and a FEATHER QUILL
- A sign showing some of the 2,300 SPECIES supported by oak trees
- A sphere of MISTLETOE with white berries
- A walking loaf of BREAD made from acorn flour
- Three homemade LIGHTNING BOLTS
- The WOODLAND BAND playing music
- MAMA RACCOON cleverly juggling acorns
- PAPA DEER'S dramatic puppet show
- A BOAT made of oak
- A wheelbarrow piled high with ACORNS
- A dazzling display of FIREWORKS
- Seven silver STARS

TIME FOR BED

The snow fell, soft and gentle,
as we tidied up the wood.
We talked about the fun we'd had;
we all felt tired, but good.

I thanked my friends for making real
the dreams inside my head.
Then winter told me: *Time to sleep!*
And so, I went to bed.

What to spot as the animals head to bed

- BEAR calling out "goodnight"
- BABY SKUNKS asleep on a pile of wrapping paper
- PAPA RABBIT and WOODPECKER holding brooms
- NANA RABBIT handing out cake
- The RACCOON FAMILY washing and drying
- The FAWNS curled up next to their planted oak saplings
- GRANDMA BAT and GRANDPA BAT fast asleep
- PAPA DEER collecting decorations
- MAMA MOUSE and PAPA MOUSE dishing out leftovers
- The SQUIRREL FAMILY burying their last acorns
- CHIPMUNKS having a bath
- MAMA FOX kissing the FOX CUBS goodnight
- The PIGEON FAMILY singing a lullaby
- GRANDPA TOAD snoring on a compost heap
- MAMA WEASEL reading a bedtime story
- BEAR'S LITTLE BROTHER and SISTER cuddling acorn toys
- The sinking SUN

So, that's the story of our Oak,

a friend so tall and true.

Now, can you go outside and find

a special tree near you... ?

TREE TRAIL

You can learn a lot about trees by focusing on one in particular and making it your special tree. Think of it like a friend – someone you visit, play with and listen to. Pick a deciduous tree (one which loses its leaves yearly, just like Grand Old Oak) near you and watch as it changes over the course of a year...

These nature-inspired illustrations were hidden in Bear's world. Did you spot them?

Turn back the pages and revisit Brown Bear Wood to try to find them.

Getting more colourful
IN SPRING

Spring flowers
Spring is the season when most deciduous trees start to produce flowers, which includes catkins. A tree's flowers come in all different shapes, sizes and colours. What are yours like? Describe them to the person you're with, then find a different type of flower on a nearby tree.

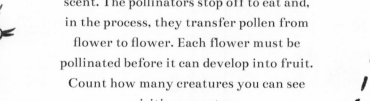

Pollinators
Flowers attract pollinators such as bees and butterflies with their colour and sweet scent. The pollinators stop off to eat and, in the process, they transfer pollen from flower to flower. Each flower must be pollinated before it can develop into fruit. Count how many creatures you can see visiting your tree.

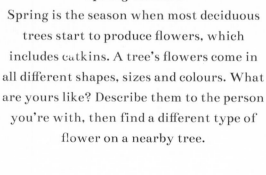

New leaves
New leaves unfurl from leaf buds, and at first they look like tiny versions of the adult leaf. A baby animal often has a different name to the adult animal, for example 'lamb', 'duckling' or 'froglet'. Can you think of a good name for a baby leaf?

Getting warmer and brighter IN SUMMER

Identify your tree

When you visit in summer, your tree's leaves will be fully grown. Look closely at the shape of your leaf. Is it oval, spear-shaped, or heart-shaped? Does it have smooth, toothed, or lobed edges? These observations will help you find the species of your tree, with some assistance from a book or website.

Fallen treasure

Acorns, which are the fruit of the oak tree, tend to mature and fall in autumn. With an adult, go outside and collect items that have fallen from trees, such as acorns, pods, helicopter seeds and pine cones. To create a sensory game, put them inside a spare sock or hat – then challenge your friends to pick out particular items!

Getting colder and darker IN AUTUMN

The full crown

Each different species of tree has a distinctive shape. Take a piece of paper and some pencils out with you and fold your paper in half. On the left-hand side, sketch the shape of the trunk, branches and leaves of your tree. Then put your paper somewhere safe, ready to get it out again in winter.

Autumn colours

Leaves are green because of chlorophyll, a substance which turns sunlight into sugary food. As the weather gets darker, the tree starts reabsorbing the chlorophyll, revealing different coloured pigments in its leaves. Take a few fallen leaves home with you and trace around them on a piece of blank paper, then colour them in.

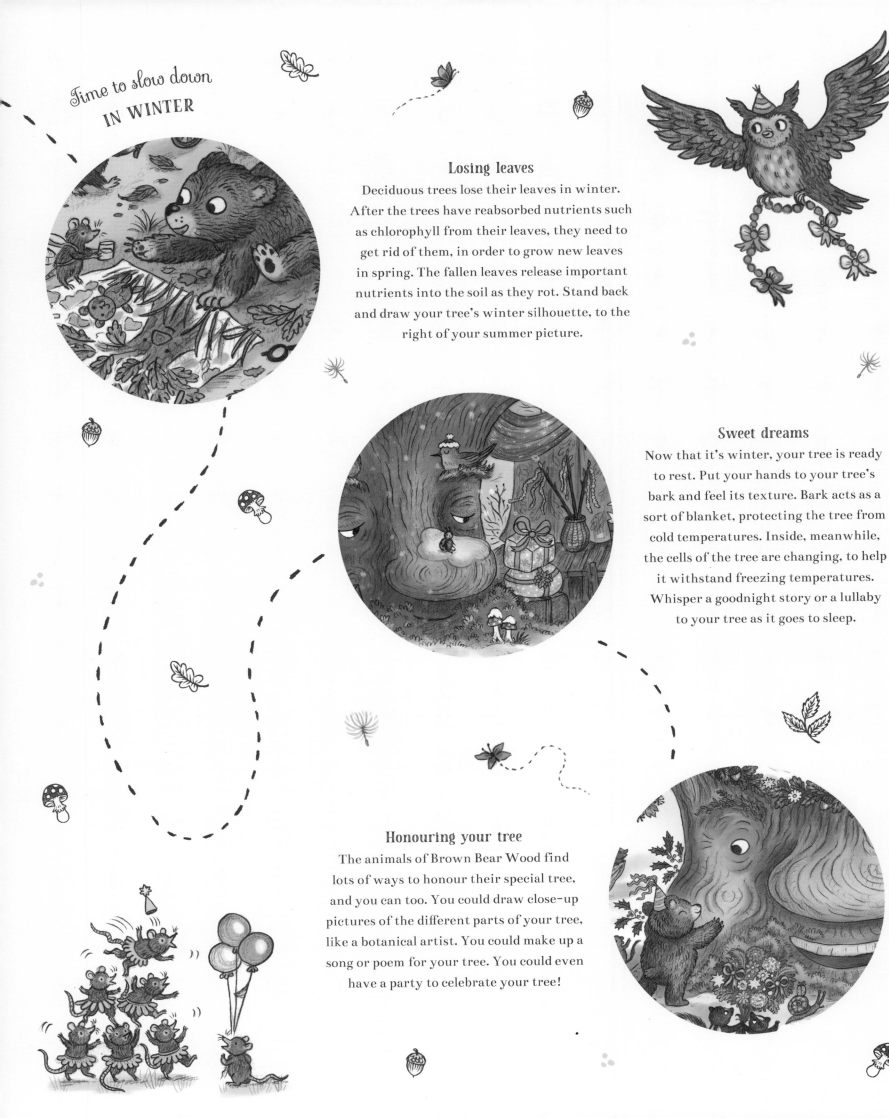

Losing leaves

Deciduous trees lose their leaves in winter. After the trees have reabsorbed nutrients such as chlorophyll from their leaves, they need to get rid of them, in order to grow new leaves in spring. The fallen leaves release important nutrients into the soil as they rot. Stand back and draw your tree's winter silhouette, to the right of your summer picture.

Sweet dreams

Now that it's winter, your tree is ready to rest. Put your hands to your tree's bark and feel its texture. Bark acts as a sort of blanket, protecting the tree from cold temperatures. Inside, meanwhile, the cells of the tree are changing, to help it withstand freezing temperatures. Whisper a goodnight story or a lullaby to your tree as it goes to sleep.

Honouring your tree

The animals of Brown Bear Wood find lots of ways to honour their special tree, and you can too. You could draw close-up pictures of the different parts of your tree, like a botanical artist. You could make up a song or poem for your tree. You could even have a party to celebrate your tree!

PARTY TIME

When you have a party, you can choose any theme you like – that's part of the fun! Here are some ideas for throwing a woodland-themed party, like the one in this book.

Sending out INVITATIONS

Bear and his friends have fun making their own invitations. You could draw some trees and plants directly onto your card or paper, or stick on **pressed flowers** and **leaves**. You could ask an adult to help you make a **potato stamp** or create a **stencil** on a woodland-themed design.

Creating the MENU

The animals of Brown Bear Wood love **berries**, so include a **seasonal selection** on your menu. Cookie cutters can shape your sandwiches into flowers. You could be imaginative with your food, too: using chocolate fingers as tree trunks, or halved tomatoes as toadstools.

Decorating a CAKE

Use **coloured sweets** to create flower patterns in the icing. Green sweets can be used to create a tree's leaves – different hues will make it look more interesting. **Desiccated coconut** mixed with green food colouring makes an effective grassy backdrop, while **grated chocolate** is good for trunks.

Making NATURAL DECORATIONS

Collect fallen flowers and leaves, and string them together to make **organic bunting**; arrange natural objects like **pine cones** in **glass jars**; you could even ask your friends to wear nature-inspired fancy dress!

Designing PARTY HATS

Party hats help to make everyone part of the theme. Pile up **long strips of thick paper**, coloured pencils, fallen leaves and flowers, animal and plant pictures from old magazines, and a few glue sticks. Ask everyone to decorate their own strip of paper, then get an adult to measure and staple the strips a round each guest's head.

Creating a SCHEDULE

Bear and his friends **plan the order** for the party in advance. You don't have to stick to your plan exactly, but it's helpful to have an idea, so you can make sure you have time for everything. Schedule your favourite things to do first so you definitely get to do them.

Playing GAMES

There are lots of ways you can give a **woodland twist** to traditional party games: tree-themed musical statues, woodland-themed charades, memory games using natural objects, or even an epic **acorn-and-spoon race**!

Planning ACTIVITIES

Absorb your guests in crafty activities such as icing leaf biscuits, making pine-cone bird feeders, or **having a paint party!**

Filling PARTY BAGS

The animals of Brown Bear Wood try not to create waste that will hang around for hundreds of years. If you would like to give out party bags or favours, some environmentally friendly options include **seeds to grow**, wooden coloured pencils, and homemade **bath bombs**.

Making the PLAYLIST

Choose an animal-themed music playlist in advance and have a wild and wonderful **disco**. You could even challenge your guests, in small groups, to create a short, themed **dance routine**.

Writing THANK YOU NOTES

If you have received a gift from someone, write them a thank you note. You could use the same **craft supplies** as you did for your invitations. It's lovely receiving an envelope with your name on, so pass on the good feelings!

TIDYING UP afterwards

There's no getting around it – this is the least enjoyable part of any party. But you can make it more fun by sticking on your party playlist and making different tasks into a **timed competition**. Ask each person helping to choose three favourite memories from the party.

Brown Bear Wood

Also available in the series

978-1-913520-47-2

978-1-913520-05-2

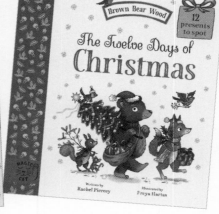

978-1-913520-48-9

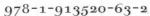

978-1-913520-63-2

978-1-913520-91-5

978-1-913520-51-9

Rachel Piercey is a poet, editor and tutor. She runs *Tyger Tyger Magazine*, an online journal of new poems for children, has co-edited three children's poetry anthologies with the Emma Press, and regularly performs and runs poetry workshops in primary schools. Rachel also has three pamphlets of poems for adults. She lives in London.

Freya Hartas is an illustrator specialising in children's books. She graduated from Falmouth University with a first class honours in BA Illustration in 2014. Alongside her magical work on the 'Brown Bear Wood' series, she is the illustrator of the bestselling 'Slow Down' series. She lives in Bristol.